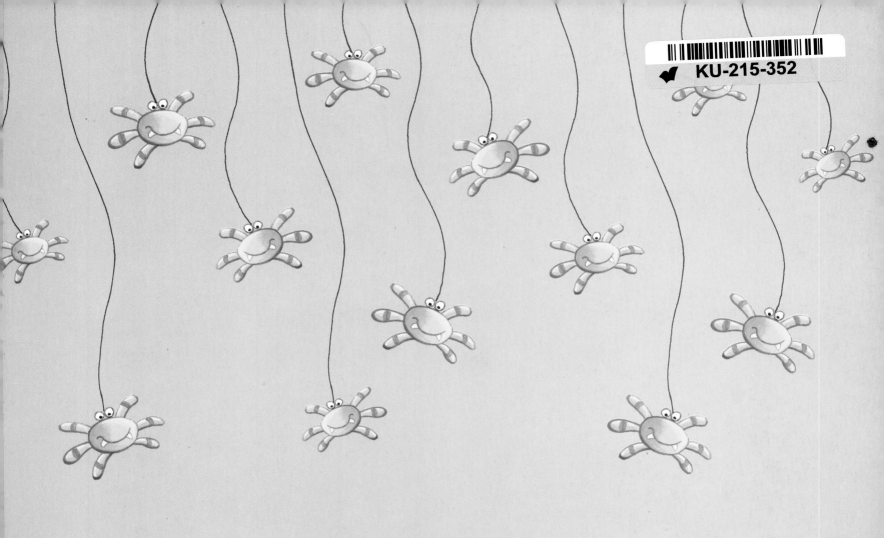

This Little Tiger book belongs to:

.................................................

.................................................

.................................................

.................................................

For Mam, Dad, Amy and Ed –
with love
EH

For Jess and Albert
PC

LITTLE TIGER PRESS
An imprint of Magi Publications
1 The Coda Centre, 189 Munster Road,
London SW6 6AW
www.littletigerpress.com

First published in Great Britain 2002

This edition published 2002

Text © 2002 Emma Harris
Illustrations © 2002 Paul Cherrill
ISBN 1 85430 837 8

A CIP catalogue for this book is available
from the British Library

Printed in Malaysia

1 3 5 7 9 10 8 6 4 2

# BEDTIME
## LITTLE MONSTERS

Emma Harris     Illustrated by Paul Cherrill

LITTLE TIGER PRESS
London

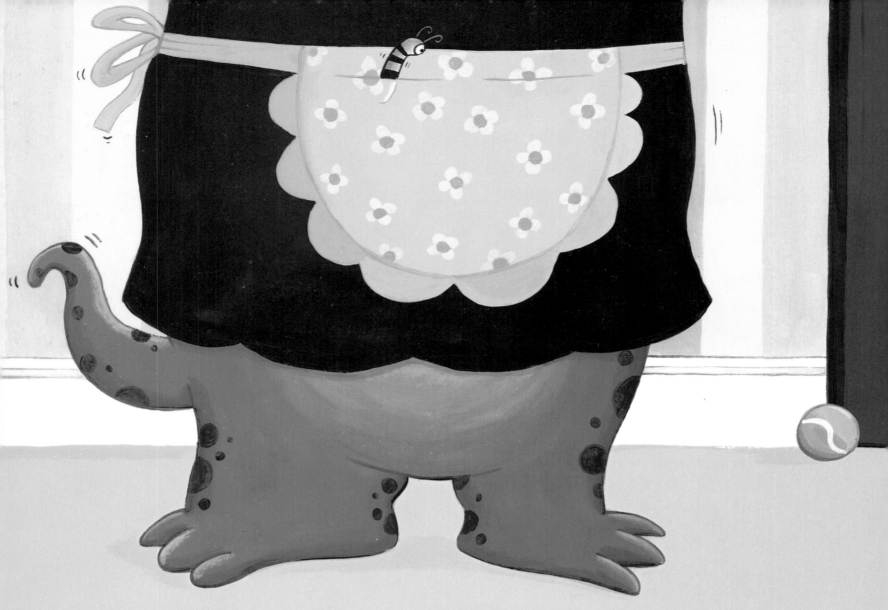

It's the Little Monsters' bedtime,
but the monsters want some fun.
So . . . scamper, scamper,
crash and bang!
Quickly off they run.

Who's that hiding
beneath the bed?

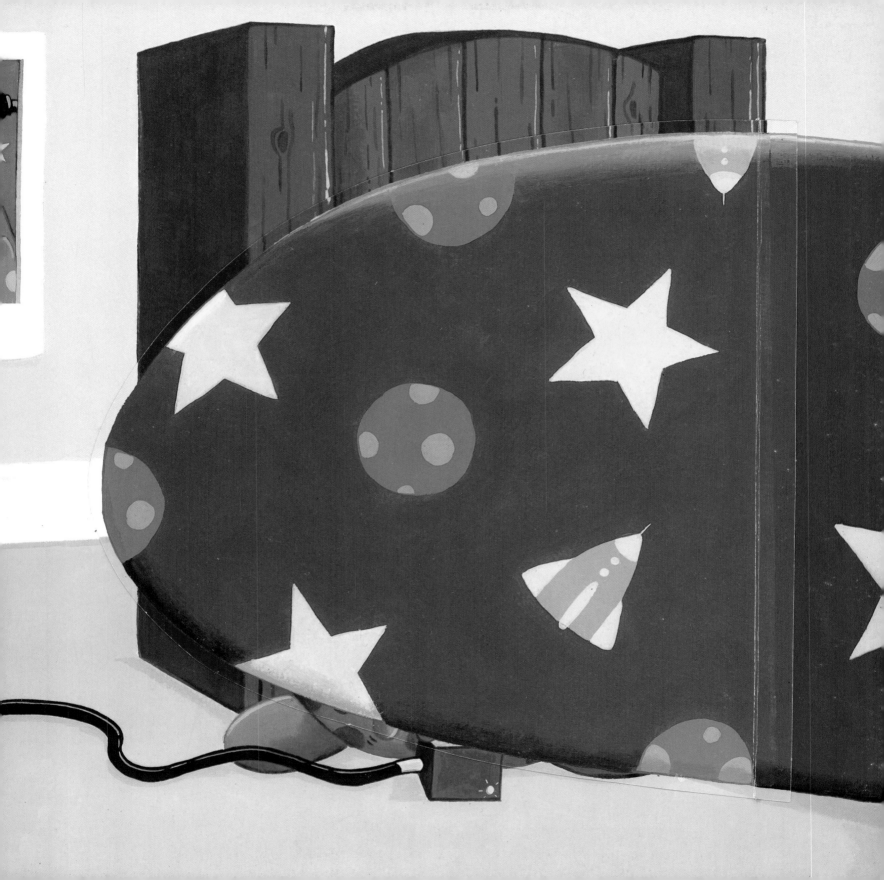

Who's in the fruit bowl?
Cheeky fellow!

Who's making bubbles
in the sink?

Who's that crashing
behind the bush?

There's someone
in the shower.
Can you guess who?

Beep! Squeak! Woof!
What's that noise?

Who's that hiding
in the TV screen?

Who's in the cupboard
having a feast?

At last the Little Monsters
have all been found.

They're tucked up in bed.
Shhh! Don't make a sound.

# More monster reads from
# Little Tiger Press

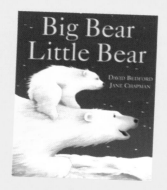
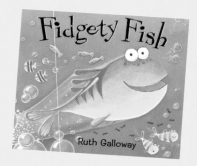

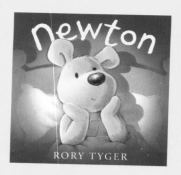

For information regarding any of the above titles or for our catalogue, please contact us:
Little Tiger Press, 1 The Coda Centre, 189 Munster Road, London SW6 6AW, UK
Tel: 020 7385 6333  Fax: 020 7385 7333  e-mail: info@littletiger.co.uk  www.littletigerpress.com